<hr>

THE DANCER AND THE ROBIN

The Shifter Season

<hr>

LAURA GREENWOOD

Visit Laura Greenwood's website at:

www.authorlauragreenwood.co.uk

Cover by Ammonia Book Covers

The Dancer and the Robin is a work of fiction. Names, characters, places, and incidents are the products of the author's imagination or are used fictitiously. Any resemblance to actual persons, living or dead, businesses, companies, events, or locales is entirely coincidental.

If you find an error, you can report it via my website. Please note that my books are written in British English: https://www.authorlauragreenwood.co.uk/p/report-error.html

To keep up to date with new releases, sales, and other updates, you can join my mailing list via my website or The Paranormal Council Reader Group on Facebook.

Blurb

When Miss Emily Falnor decides to pay a surprise visit to her sister in time for the Annual Shifter Yuletide Ball, the last thing she expects is to fall in love.

The dashing Mr William Crestfellow never planned to be swept off his feet when he visits his closest friend, but the moment he meets Miss Falnor, he knows that he has lost his heart for good.

While Emily's sister seems intent on stopping the match, a masquerade ball provides the perfect opportunity for the two avian shifters to meet without anyone becoming wiser...

-

The Dancer and the Robin is a paranormal Regency romance with falcon and robin shifters. It is a Shifter Season short story. It has an m/f romance and is Emily and William's complete story.

Chapter 1

EMILY

The cool crisp air ruffles my feathers as I soar through the air and towards the large house my sister now calls home. It will be strange to refer to her as *Your Grace*, though I suppose I will only be required to do that when we are amongst other company. When we are alone, she will solely be Mary, just as she always has been.

I spot the roof I'm looking for, and the roost on top of it just waiting for my arrival. Not that Mary is actually aware of it, but she will be soon enough, and we both know she wouldn't turn her baby sister away, even if she doesn't approve of me flying this late at night.

I swoop down and enter the roost through the large open window, glad to find that no one else seems to have had the same idea about using it. That should give me some privacy, which is particularly important given that I don't currently have any of my belongings with me. I've had them sent to the house, but only so that they would arrive after me.

I land in the middle of the floor and instantly call a shift. My body changes quickly, growing in size and changing in shape. It never ceases to amaze me how my human form can be contained in that of a falcon, especially given the size difference. But I suspect those kinds of mysteries are for people much smarter than I to unravel. Perhaps Mary and her new husband have a theory.

A pile of rich-looking fabric catches my eye and a small smile lifts at the corners of my lips. I should have known that Mary would always make sure the roost has clothing in case she returns and is of need of it. And luck would have it that we are the same height.

A sharp breeze through the small window sends a shiver down my spine. I take hold of the chemise from the pile and put it on quickly, following it with the dress. Neither are made of thick enough fabric to withstand the cold for long, but it is of no matter.

Satisfied that I am not about to give any of the servants a shock they do not wish to see, I open the door. A small bell rings out through the quiet of the evening, causing me to wince. I had hoped not to draw any attention to myself until I have had a chance to speak with Mary. While I do not believe her husband will throw me from his home, I can not pretend to know him at all beyond what my sister has told me in her letters.

Footsteps sound down the hall from me and a man with dark hair and a face I vaguely recognise comes into view.

He frowns when he sees me. "Mary?"

"No, Your Grace," I say, dipping into a curtsy. "I'm her sister. Miss Emily Falnor. I regret that I was not able to come to your wedding, I was attending on a distant aunt." Which is my way of saying that I was more or less held hostage by her, but it is best if he does not know the complexities of my situation. Perhaps Mary has already told him of it, but I do not wish to betray her confidence if she has not.

"Good evening, Miss Falnor, I will inform the Duchess of your arrival," he says, regaining his composure with surprising speed.

"There's no need," Mary's voice says from behind him. "I am here." She touches her husband's arm with evident affection.

"Mary," I say.

"Emily, I wasn't expecting you," she responds with caution. "I shall call for some tea. And you must stay the night, it is far too cold for you to fly all that way tonight."

"I did not intend to return until the New Year," I respond, ignoring the small part of me that is screaming about how ridiculous my desire truly is.

Her eyes widen. "I see."

"I shall call the servants to prepare a room and deliver tea to your drawing room," the Duke tells my sister.

She smiles gratefully at him. "Thank you, Stephen," she whispers.

The smile he gives her feels as if it is not for my eyes.

My sister doesn't say a word as she waits for him to leave, which makes me certain that I am in great trouble for my arrival.

"I was not expecting you." The expression on her face is one that I suspect is reserved for me alone. And given the situation, I probably deserve it. And the reminder that I've turned up unannounced.

"No."

She lets out a loud sigh. "I don't suppose that

anything will convince you to leave now that you are here."

"You know that it will not."

"What did our aunt do now?" She gestures for me to fall into step beside her.

"She is attempting to marry me off to the local vicar."

Mary grimaces. "That seems like a poor choice."

"It makes me wonder what she has promised him in the past to be going through with it. You'd believe that she would aim higher considering your marriage."

Mary lets out a soft laugh. "You know that she disapproves because of how I met Stephen."

"A duke is still a duke, even if he does have interesting pastimes."

"Is that why you are here?" she asks. "Do you wish for us to try and extract you from our aunt's care? I do not believe that Father's will left much room for that."

"It was not my intention," I admit. "Though now you suggest it, I must admit it is a tempting offer."

"And one that I have already asked the Duke to look into," she promises me. "His lawyers are hoping to make an argument for the transfer of your guardianship, though I fear that our aunt won't let you go without a fight."

"She likes the money," I mutter.

"Yes. But perhaps that allows us a simple way around it. If money is what she desires, then we have plenty of it."

"I suppose marriage would be an easy way out of it."

"You can not marry simply to escape from our aunt," Mary says firmly.

"And what reason should I marry? Financial security and freedom both seem to be good choices, particularly when the alternative is that I marry the local vicar who I do not know. Is he even a shifter? That is how little knowledge I have of him."

"Oh, Emily," she says softly. "You do not need to marry for either of those reasons, you should marry because your heart tells you that it is time."

"That is rather easy for you to say, your heart brought you to a duke."

"If you think me at all swayed by Stephen's rank, then I fear you do not know me well at all, sister."

"That's not what I meant and you know it."

She sighs. "Why are you really here, Emily? If

you wished to escape our aunt, you would simply have sent me a letter to ask if you could visit, which forces me to believe that you are here for a reason I may not be best pleased about." She opens a door for me and gestures for me to head inside the room.

The moment I do, it becomes clear that it is for her private use. Everything about the room says that it belongs to Mary, from the abandoned books on one of the chaises, to the scattered pages on the desk, and the multitude of mostly-used candles scattered around the room. Each of them having been used to a point and then forgotten about as she moves on to the next thing that interests her. The sight of it brings a smile to my face.

"Emily," Mary says, recalling my attention to her.

"I wish to attend the Shifter Yuletide Ball," she says.

"No."

"Whyever not? I've been presented, I'm of good descent, and my sister is a Duchess."

"All reasons why you shouldn't attend. What if someone decides to take advantage of you?"

I raise an eyebrow. "I'm perfectly capable of looking after myself, Mary," I remind her.

She sighs. "You're going to be insufferable if I say no, aren't you?"

"You know me well, sister."

She lets out a loud sigh that makes me certain that she is going to agree, even if she doesn't wish to.

"Very well. I'll set up an appointment with the modiste. There isn't much time to get you a dress for the ball, but considering you're wearing one of mine right now, I don't see that we have much choice," she says.

"I am having a trunk delivered."

"I doubt that anything in it will be suitable. I'll make the appointment."

A wide smile spreads over my face. "Thank you, Mary. You won't regret saying yes."

She lets out a small chuckle. "Somehow, I doubt that."

Perhaps she's right. I am known for getting myself into small spots of trouble. But I'm determined to prove Mary wrong and that allowing me to attend is the right thing for me.

Chapter 2

WILLIAM

The threat of snow hangs in the air like it often does this time of year, and I find myself welcoming it with open arms. There's always something satisfying about the crisp layer of white it creates. The pristineness makes me long to head outside in my shifted form and make my way through it, leaving small footprints in my wake.

I tug on the reins and direct my horse towards the stables where I know a servant will be waiting for me to arrive so they can tend to her. Just one of the many advantages of arriving at my friend's home instead of my father's. I know that I'm supposed to want to spend the Yuletide season with him and his new wife, but I can't bring myself to, not with how miserable she likes to try and make me.

And my sister. Thankfully, Flora has an invitation to spend the season with friends of her own, meaning that I'm free to do as I wish myself.

I pull Bessie to a stop and dismount, patting her neck in gratitude as I hand her off to the waiting groom. I know he'll take good care of her, and I've spent enough time at Clawdon's manor to know that they'll have Bessie's favourite treats waiting for her.

I head towards the front door, half surprised that my old school friend isn't already waiting outside to greet me. Perhaps he's more interested in spending time with his new wife. I suppose in his position I might be tempted to do the same, especially as he spoke in his letters of the two of them sharing many of the same interests.

The doorman nods to me as I pass. "His Grace is in the second parlour, sir."

"Thank you, Prowly."

I make my way swiftly to the parlour, not bothering to change into anything more suited for calling on a friend. I believe that Clawdon and I have known one another long enough that he can see me in my riding clothes.

The moment I enter the room, I start questioning my decision as there's one thing I failed to take into account.

There's now a Duchess of Clawdon, and this is the first time I'm going to meet her.

Two women rise to their feet as I enter, followed by my friend.

"Crestfellow, how are you?" he asks, embracing me and patting me on the back.

"Better now I'm amongst friends," I respond to the Duke.

He steps back and smiles warmly. "Please allow me to introduce the Duchess to you," he says, gesturing to the closer of the two women.

"Your Grace," I say with a nod of my head.

"Mr Crestfellow, I've heard much about you," the brunette responds with a slight hint of amusement in her voice.

"I dread to think what the Duke has told you of me."

"Only good things," she promises.

"I'm not sure I believe you."

A slight smirk pulls at the side of her lips.

"And this is the Duchess' sister," Clawdon says, gesturing to the other woman.

"Miss Emily Falnor," she says, dipping into a curtsy.

"Mr William Crestfellow," I respond with a bow of my head.

"Do you enjoy riding, Mr Crestfellow?" she asks as she takes a seat on one of the chaises.

"I do." I sit on the other end, being careful to keep a respectful distance between us. The last thing I want is to make anyone uncomfortable, or introduce a hint of impropriety.

"Do you have a favourite horse?"

"I only have one. She's in the stables at the moment."

"I would like to meet her, if you don't mind?"

"Emily!" the Duchess scolds.

"I am merely asking to see a horse, Mary, I don't see any problem with that," Miss Falnor replies in a matter-of-fact tone. "I'm sure Mr Crestfellow will be willing to let you accompany us so you can be sure there's no impropriety."

"I would be horrified should he not," the Duchess responds.

"I would never dream of putting any lady in a compromising position," I assure the Duchess.

"He would not," Clawdon assures her.

"Perhaps it is not Mr Crestfellow I fear for," the Duchess mutters.

I raise an eyebrow while Miss Falnor smothers a laugh.

"She believes I have a penchant for getting myself in trouble," she supplies by way of explanation.

"I'm certain that isn't the case."

"Oh, it is," she responds. "I try not to, but trouble always seems to find me." Her lips quirk up into a knowing smile, almost as if she's issuing some kind of challenge when it comes to what she can get up to.

I swallow hard. I have to admit that there's something about her that makes me want to break all kinds of rules. Not just those of propriety either. I don't know precisely what it is, but I feel as if she has an air about her that could make anyone do anything.

The Duchess clears her throat. "You'll have to excuse us, gentlemen, or we're going to be late for our appointment with the modiste."

"Ah, my dress for the ball," Miss Falnor says with a sparkle of excitement in her eyes. "Will you be attending, Mr Crestfellow?"

"Which ball would that be, Miss Falnor?" I respond.

"The Shifter Yuletide Ball, is there any other this time of year?"

"I suspect there are plenty."

"Yes, but they're mixed with humans. This is *the* ball for shifters." She pauses as if realising that no one has made it clear that I am one. She looks down sweetly, then back up as if she's been caught. "You are aware of the ball, are you not?"

I'm starting to understand what the Duchess is worried about. I suspect the concern is all too valid. "I'm aware of the ball."

"And you will be attending?"

"I have an invitation, though in truth I have not decided whether to attend or not."

"Oh, but you should. There will be dancing, and so much fun. We don't even have to abide by the rules because no one will know who we are." Her excitement for the event is clear just from the way she speaks of it, and a part of me wishes to accept the invitation right now.

"*I* will know who you are," the Duchess mutters.

Miss Falnor cocks her head to the side as if she's heard, but pays no heed to her sister's words.

"We should go, Emily," the Duchess says firmly.

She gets to her feet and nods to Clawdon and me in turn. "Your Grace, Mr Crestfellow."

Miss Falnor sighs and gets to her feet. "Very well. I shall take my leave. Your Grace." She dips her head to the Duke, then turns to me. "Mr Crestfellow, it has been a pleasure, I hope we can get to know one another better soon." She holds out her hand to me.

My instincts kick in and I take it, raising it to my lips and kissing the back of her gloved hand.

I look up and meet her gaze, finding more than a little interest lingering in them.

It would certainly seem that the new Duchess of Clawdon is correct, her sister has a knack for getting into trouble.

And I fear I'm already caught within its grasp too.

Chapter 3

EMILY

The seamstresses flit in and out of the fitting room at the back of the modiste, and I have to admit feeling a twinge of guilt that I'm causing them so much last-minute work just because I decided to show up unannounced and without anything to wear to the ball I want to attend.

But what else could I have done? If I had written and asked, Mary would have said no and told me that I should wait another few years. Or until I'm married, which doesn't sound nearly so good.

The head seamstress enters the room and heads straight towards my sister, whispering something to her.

Mary offers the woman a reassuring smile. "Add it to my account, whatever you need."

The seamstress' eyes widen. "Are you sure, Your Grace? It is quite a sum."

"I'm certain," Mary responds. "We've requested the near-impossible from you, we're willing to pay for that."

"Thank you, Your Grace." She dips into a curtsy and hurries from the room.

"It surprises me that you're showing off your new funds so easily," I say to Mary.

She shoots me a withering look. "I'm not showing them off, I'm paying for the service that you've required us to need, there's a difference."

"I suppose there is from your side. To others, perhaps not."

"Unfortunately, one of the downsides of being a Duchess is that I'm required to act as if I have money."

"Because you do."

"My husband does," she corrects me. "What I have is very little compared to his wealth. And I'm lucky that Father insisted on the provision in his will that means I keep my portion of our inheritance myself despite having married."

"And are we spending yours or His Grace's money today?"

"We should be spending yours," she mutters.

"You know that's not an option. Our aunt..."

"Yes. I'm aware that she's stopped your access to it and that's why you felt the need to come here in the first place. The Duke has his lawyers working on the situation."

I let out a sigh of relief. "Thank you."

Her expression softens. "You're welcome. I don't wish for you to remain living with our aunt if that is not where you wish to be."

"Nor do you want me to be here and attending the Shifter Yuletide Ball."

She lets out a small laugh. "That's because I know you, Emily. We're both well aware that you will almost certainly get yourself into a troublesome situation at the ball."

"Then I shall be additionally relieved that my sister is not only particularly clever, but also a Duchess. I can see how both of those things can be useful when one is attempting to stay out of trouble."

"Staying out of it seems to be something you're incapable of. And you should be wary. There are some situations even the Duke's connections won't be able to get you out of," she warns.

"I promise I'll try to stay away from those."

"You should stay away from any situation that could get you into trouble," she counters. "And that includes Mr Crestfellow."

I frown, trying to think why that would be the case. He seems like a perfectly charming fellow, and someone who she would wish me to spend time with.

Before I can ask her about it, one of the seamstresses enters the room and gestures for me to turn around.

I do as instructed and hold out my arms while she drapes tawny fabric over my shoulders.

"Is this the right colour?" I ask. "I feel like it should be brighter."

"Are you trying to tell me you decided to attend the ball without learning about it?" There's a hint of amusement in Mary's voice. "It is tradition to wear something that represents your shifter side."

"I thought it was a masquerade."

"It is."

"Then surely displaying what creature we can transform into would rather defeat the point of not being able to tell who someone is."

"There are nearly three dozen falcon shifter families with children our age, I suspect you will be fine." She nods to the seamstress to continue. From the way she's talking so openly, I have to assume we're in a supernatural modiste. Which I suppose makes sense when elaborate costumes are apparently needed.

"Even so, I don't believe it will take too much to discover someone's identity."

"Then perhaps you should see it as motivation to behave." The stern look she gives me would be enough to make most people listen to her. But I can't help it. I know better than to get myself into situations that my sister disapproves of, but that doesn't seem to be enough to stop it from happening.

The seamstress takes her leave, probably to cut some pieces for the dress.

"Why do I need to stay away from Mr Crestfellow?" I ask the moment she's gone.

Surprise flits over Mary's face, as if she expected me to move on from her statement and not return from it. "He is my husband's oldest friend, I won't have you ruining their friendship."

"Is that the only reason?"

"Do I need another one? I wish to protect my husband."

"I thought you were going to tell me of some horrible misdeed or sleight that Mr Crestfellow had committed." I have to admit that there is a small part of me that is more intrigued by Mr Crestfellow than before. If my sister disapproves of my possible interest in him, then it makes me wish to know him more.

Though that was something I had already been considering. I liked the way he held himself earlier, though one meeting is hardly enough to judge a person on. I shall endeavour to uncover all of his secrets at our next one, which I'm sure won't be far away considering we're both guests at Mary and her husband's manor.

"What are you thinking?" Mary asks, a note of suspicion in her voice. "I hate it when you get that look in your eye."

"Just considering the ways in which I can make myself a most pleasant guest for you and your dear husband." It's a lie, and I'm certain she's aware of as much.

Thankfully, she makes a soft humming noise and nods. Whether she believes me or not, she's choosing to let the subject drop.

And I'm not going to say anything to change that, not when I might have some peace for the rest of my fitting.

Chapter 4

EMILY

I touch the side of my mask, wondering how well it truly conceals my identity, particularly when it is combined by the exquisite gown that proclaims for all to see that I am a falcon shifter. I suppose it is as Mary said, there are several falcon shifter families in attendance this evening, including that of her husband.

And that is without considering the number of other bird shifters in attendance. Everywhere I look there seem to be hints of plumage, and I have to admit to feeling a slight twinge of jealousy as a couple adorned in bright blues and peacock feathers dance past us. Why do I have such dull plumage compared to theirs?

I touch the large feather adorning the neckline of my dress. I suppose it is spectacular in its own way, even if it is not as colourful as those belonging to the peafowl.

Snowflakes flutter down from the ceiling, vanishing before they touch the heads of the crowd.

"How?" I whisper.

"It was probably a witch," Mary says from beside me. "I heard they wished to make the ball even more spectacular than those that Lady Ferrington holds, and for that, they needed something spectacular."

"They've succeeded. I believe the only thing that would be better is if it was real snow."

"Pray it waits until we've returned to the manor and doesn't trap us all here," she mutters.

"Or pray that it does and we can all have a ball that extends through until dawn."

"The ball already goes until dawn," she points out.

"Well, longer then. You know, you really should try having fun more often, Mary. It's a wonder you ended up married at all."

She raises an eyebrow. "Need I remind you that I met the Duke through being serious? Perhaps that is something *you* should try."

I let out a loud sigh. "I'm sorry, that was unreasonable of me. We're supposed to be enjoying ourselves this evening. Why don't you tell me who is who?"

"I thought you'd been to balls?"

"Only the most boring ones. You know what our aunt is like, she only wants me to attend the ones where she can sit with her friends, and she doesn't have many of those."

"Hmm, fair point." She scans the room and nods towards a copper-haired woman with a dappled brown and white mask. "That's Lady Ferrington over there, with the Baron next to her, I believe."

"That's the cousin of her late husband?"

"Ah, your gossip has fallen behind in the country," she responds with amusement. "The Baron is her current husband. But yes, he's a distant cousin of her first."

"How scandalous."

"Hardly. It was no secret around the ton that Lady Ferrington's first marriage was a loveless one."

"And now?"

"A love match, by all accounts," Mary responds. "As was the marriage of the Viscount Renarton. He's there with his wife." She points out a couple dressed in deep orange with ears above their heads. Even if I didn't already know that the Renarton line belongs to fox shifters, I'd be able to tell from their outfits.

"I have to say I'm surprised at your knowledge of gossip," I admit. "I would have thought you were too busy reading your books to notice these things."

"I can have more than one interest," she corrects me. "Though I'll admit I've mostly been making myself learn these things because I'm expected to know them. I have to be aware of who is connected to who. Like Lady Renarton is good friends with Mrs Peabury. If I need an introduction or an invitation from someone, then I simply have to work out who they themselves know, and go from there."

"It sounds awfully complicated," I admit.

"Which is why when I entered the marriage market, I never intended to find myself a husband with so much rank and status. There are many advantages to being a Duchess, and even more to having married the man I love, but I sometimes wish we were less important in the grand scheme of things."

"Oh, Mary, I had no idea."

"Why would you? It isn't something I wish to put into writing. But it does make me glad that you're here so I can talk to someone I trust about it."

"You can always confide in me," I promise, meaning the words. I suppose I haven't given much thought to how difficult it must have been for Mary to make the transition from a relative nobody, to one of the most powerful ladies in the room, especially when she's never been one for wanting the attention.

"Thank you, Emily. I truly am glad you're here to share this with me."

"Me too," I assure her, hoping this means that she's going to be a little less frustrated with me from now on.

Our moment is interrupted by a lady with a bright white dress adorned with feathers approaching. She smiles widely at my sister. "Your Grace," she says in a friendly tone.

Mary lets out a small chuckle. "I told you that you didn't need to call me that." She turns to me. "I believe that you have met Lady Cygnus before, but when she went by Miss Swanley."

Recognition dawns on me as I put together my

memories of Mary's close friend who was always getting all of the attention at events, and the elegant woman in front of me. I used to idolise her when I was younger for the easy way she had with just about everyone.

"Always a pleasure to see you again, Miss Emily."

"Likewise, Lady Cygnus." Somehow, I believe that there has to be a story behind how such a flirtatious free spirit ended up married, and happily from her demeanour.

"Have you seen Georgiana yet?" Lady Cygnus asks.

Mary shakes her head. "I'm sure she'll be arriving soon."

My attention fades, not in the slightest bit interested in the whereabouts of my sister's friend. My gaze lands on a handsome gentleman across the room. Or at least I presume that he's handsome. He's tall, with dark hair, and a bright red waistcoat under a dark brown jacket. If I'm to guess what he is from the way he's dressed, I'd have to say a robin. Though of course there is a chance that he's chosen not to attend under his shifter side's colours. I'm sure there are plenty of people in the room using that tactic as misdirection to divert attention away from their identity.

Would it be entirely improper of me to head in his direction and strike up a conversation? Under normal circumstances, I would need to be formally introduced, but the Shifter Yuletide Ball isn't the usual kind. Here, anyone can be anybody.

And with that comes the chance to break free of the constraints placed upon me.

I glance at Mary to make sure she isn't paying any attention to me. She's deep in conversation with Lady Cygnus, giving me an excellent chance to make my escape.

I take a step in the direction of the handsome stranger, only for a gentleman wearing an outrageous orange jacket to step between us.

"May I have the honour of this dance, My Lady?" he asks.

"Who says I am a lady?" I ask in response.

He chuckles. "When a gentleman has no way of knowing an identity, it is always better to assume that someone is a lady."

"Well said, My Lord. And deserving of a dance, I would think." I offer him my hand, not just because I want to, or because it is technically improper for me to reject a gentleman's request for a dance when I have not yet been promised to another, but because it is a way of escaping Mary's attention that even she will be unable to argue with.

I let him whisk me onto the dancefloor, intent on enjoying every moment of dancing with a stranger.

Chapter 5

WILLIAM

No matter where I am in the room, my gaze keeps getting pulled back to the same woman. I think it's the way she laughs and seems to have an almost reckless enjoyment about her.

It's captivating in a way that I've never experienced before.

The current set ends and she says something to her partner, presumably thanking him for the dance. I watch as she turns to make her way to the refreshments table and see my chance at managing to strike up a conversation with her. So far, every time I've tried, someone else has gotten there before me.

I'm clearly not the only one who can sense her

enjoyment of the evening and wishes for some part of it.

"My Lady," I say to get her attention.

She turns to face me, her eyes widening. "Why, Lord Robin Redbreast, how good to finally get to meet you."

The moment she speaks, the familiarity in the way she moves clicks into place. No wonder I've been finding myself drawn to her, just like I have every other time we've crossed paths in the Duke's manor.

"You've been watching for me?" I ask, surprised at how forward she's being. Either she's yet to recognise me, or doesn't wish to acknowledge that she has. Which is fair when I'm choosing to do the same.

"Your waistcoat is rather striking, I wager that it's drawn the attention of just about every lady in the room. And some of the gentlemen, if I were to hazard a guess."

I raise an eyebrow. "I do believe that's a rather improper thing to say."

She lets out a small laugh and picks up a glass of lemonade. "I do believe that the purpose of a masquerade is that we can all say the improper things that are on our minds with no risk of recrimination."

"I'm sure your...chaperone would say differently." I catch myself almost saying sister. I'm not sure whether it is me, or Miss Falnor that the Duchess doesn't trust, but she certainly seems to have made coming between us an art form. I'm half-surprised that she hasn't managed to intercede now.

"My chaperone is thankfully occupied by her husband. I believe they headed to the gardens in order to *take in the air*, though I'm almost certain that is not what they meant."

I let out an amused laugh. "And what do you suppose they meant?"

"Things that I don't believe I'm supposed to be aware of, and so I shall do the proper thing and not share them with you."

"Ah, but was it not you who said that the masquerade is an excuse for us all to say the things that are on our minds but would be improper to say any other time." I can feel the satisfied smirk on my face, but I can't do anything to stop it, nor do I wish to. This is the effect that Miss Falnor has had on me even after a few brief meetings.

"Then perhaps if you impress me on the dancefloor, I might consider inviting you on a walk myself and then you will find out."

I stare at her, completely lost for words. I can't tell if she knows what she's suggesting, or if she's trying to pretend she does in order to sound worldly.

"I would not wish to ruin you."

"Then don't."

"I don't believe it's as simple as that."

"Tonight, it is." She drinks her lemonade and sets it down on the table. "Are you going to ask me to dance?"

"I believe you just did that for me."

"I wouldn't dream of taking up your valuable time if you do not wish to."

I hold out my arm. "Any time spent with you will be worth it."

"You don't even know me."

"That is why I wish to spend time with you," I point out as I lead her onto the dancefloor and to the bottom of the set. "Is that not why we dance at these events? Aren't you supposed to be using the dances to search for a husband?"

"Perhaps I'm not in need of one. Or if I am, maybe I desire more than good conversation and excellent dance skills."

"What more is there?"

"If that question is serious, then I believe the answer is that you do not meet my requirements."

I chuckle. She's certainly bold, though I'm not entirely sure that's because of the mask. "Is it a title you seek?"

"No, that is not important to me."

"Then a fortune," I guess.

"I have money of my own," she replies. "In theory."

"In theory?" I echo.

She sighs. "When Father died, he left me an inheritance that will remain in my care and not that of any husband, current or future. Unfortunately, my aunt does not wish to part with it, even though she can not spend it." For a moment, her entire demeanour becomes more serious.

"Ah, I can see how that could be a potential issue."

"It is of no matter. My sister's new husband is looking into it for me, and you should forget I ever said a word on the matter."

"And pray tell who is your sister's husband?" I ask.

Her eyes widen, seemingly as she realises that she's said something that could lead someone to work out who she is. "His name is unimportant, but he is not."

I let out a soft chuckle. That's certainly one way of describing a Duke.

"What of you, what do you look for in a wife? Beauty and compliance, most likely."

"Who is it that once said that beauty is in the eye of the beholder?"

"That would be a question for my sister," she responds. "Though your suggestion would imply that you believe at least some women to be ugly."

"That could not be further from the truth," I assure her quickly. "I believe that every woman is beautiful in her own way."

"Mmm. You have said nothing about the compliance you would expect from a wife."

"I know that it is unseemly, and perhaps I should not admit it to a near stranger, but I wish for my future marriage to be a partnership, not a matter of one party being compliant to the other."

She raises an eyebrow. "An unusual stance. And clever confirmation that you are yet to find your wife. Should I expect a proposal?"

"We should at least dance with one another first," I point out, though I won't deny that there is a part of me that wishes it is something I could consider. But I could not do that to Clawdon. Nor to his new wife.

And more importantly, it would not be fair to either of us. While I'm certainly enjoying Miss Falnor's company, I need more than one conversation to know if she is a good fit for me, and I for her, even if she is proving to have a fast wit and strong opinions.

We're stopped from talking further by the start of the dance, our concentration needed for focusing on where we should be putting our feet, particularly when there are fabric wings and tails to take into consideration that aren't normally part of the routine.

I suppose that's just one of the perils of a shifters-only masquerade ball.

Falling for a falcon shifter I barely know may be another.

Chapter 6

EMILY

The dance comes to an end, and I curtsy low to Mr Crestfellow, not that I'm supposed to know who he is. I suppose this is a side of the masquerade that I hadn't considered. I know who it is I'm dancing with, but I get to pretend that I don't. It gives me a chance to properly get to know the gentleman in a way I wouldn't be able to.

"Would you care for another dance?" Mr Crestfellow asks.

I raise an eyebrow. "Would that not imply that we're serious about courting?"

"I believe that would be the case at any usual ball, but that is not where we are tonight," he points out, a mischievous grin on his face.

"Ah, so you're a man who likes to break the rules."

"Only bend them," he counters. "And only when there is a beautiful dance partner involved."

"So now I am beautiful."

"I never said that you weren't," he points out. "Simply that I thought all ladies were beautiful."

"Perhaps I'm starting to believe you. Unfortunately, I do believe that I am tired from all the dancing, perhaps a walk might be in order instead?"

"Would you like me to accompany you?"

My lips curve up into a mischievous smile. "I was very much hoping that you would, Lord Redbreast."

"Is that what you're going to call me now?"

"Would you prefer I chose something else?" I ask.

For a moment, I think he's about to ask me to call him by his given name, but he shakes his head. "And what should I call you?"

"That is your choice. I believe it's only fair when I am the one who gave you a name."

He chuckles and offers me his arm.

I slip my own through it and rest my gloved hand on his sleeve.

"I believe I shall call you Lady Wit."

"Ah, you're not choosing any of my shifter qualities then."

"In truth, I do not know how to tell birds of prey apart. You could be an owl, a hawk, a kite, or an eagle for all I know."

"I am none of those things."

We easily fall into step beside one another as we make our way through the crowded ballroom and towards the doors opening out into the gardens. Despite the chill in the air, there's a steady stream of people coming and going, making me fear that we may not have the privacy I wish for once we are out there.

"I would suggest that you are not dressed as your shifter at all, but I don't feel that would be the case."

"My sister chose my gown," I admit. "I did not realise that people chose to come as their animal to a ball such as this."

"I believe many feel like it is their only chance to. Most people never shift in front of those who are not their family, so this is a chance to express themselves."

"Perhaps that is true, but surely I am more than a falcon shifter? And you are more than a robin."

A small smile tugs at the corners of his lips.

Worry cascades through me as I wonder about whether I've said too much and revealed who I am. But I take a deep breath and remind myself that it would take far more than an offhand comment for him to be able to put the pieces together, especially when he may not even be very aware of the falcon-shifting families and how many children each of them has. I could be any number of people.

"Do you like to fly?" he asks.

"That would be a question that implies I *am* simply a bird shifter."

"Not at all, I find that one's fondness for flying has nothing to do with one's capability."

I let out a small laugh. "I love flying. It makes me feel free. What about you?"

"Not so much. I prefer hopping along the ground. I'm sure you know the way that robins do."

"So you are a robin?" I may know that he is Mr Crestfellow, but Mary has refused to tell me anything about him. I don't think she realises that it's only made him that much more mysterious and enticing to me. Though with how easy it seems to be for me to hold a conversation with him, I may start to think that a good thing.

"I am. Red happens to look particularly good on me."

"It does. Though without being able to see your entire face, that might be harder to ascertain."

He chuckles. "Are you asking me to unmask before the end of the ball?"

"Only if you wish to find me again, Lord Redbreast."

"I don't believe that will be a problem, Lady Wit. I'm certain I shall know you the moment you walk into the same room as I'm in." There's a hint of amusement in his tone that makes me believe he knows precisely when that is going to be, and that he will make sure the opportunity does not go to waste.

We step through the open doors and out into the gardens. Torches light the path, and there's the faint sound of laughter even over the music drifting from the ballroom.

"Sadly, I do not believe we are alone enough for you to unmask," I say, not expecting how much disappointment there is within me at that. I already know who is behind the mask, so why is it so important to me that he takes it off?

"There are more private places we can go," he says in a low voice.

"If you're suggesting a retiring room, then I

must say that your instincts are incorrect. People are caught there far too often."

"Do you not wish to be caught with me, Lady Wit?"

"How can I when we have only just met? Now perhaps in five or six balls time, I may feel rather differently."

"I shall endeavour to make it so. But I wasn't referring to a retiring room. Did you know they have a maze here?"

"I did not."

"There are many hidden places within."

"I could be persuaded," I respond, knowing that this is probably one of the most reckless things I've ever done. But it feels so right.

And who am I to ignore the feeling?

Chapter 7

EMILY

At first, the maze is much darker than the path outside, but soon the moonlight takes over, and the enhancements to my vision being a falcon shifter give me kick in and I am able to see everything around me with surprising clarity.

My heart pounds as we round a corner, taking us further away from anyone else enjoying the gardens. This is reckless.

This is going to cause more trouble than even I want to.

And yet I can't stop.

"Is here private enough for you to unmask, Lord Redbreast?" I ask, trying not to let myself sound too out of breath lest he interpret it incorrectly.

"Perhaps."

I turn to face him, only realising once I do that we're very close together. I place my hand on his chest to steady myself. His heart is pounding as fast as mine, and I look up to find his gaze boring into me.

My attention flicks to his lips, and I find myself wondering what they taste like.

I want to push the thought away, but it won't leave.

"I should tell you my name," I whisper.

"I know your name," he responds, his voice low and inviting. "I've known from the moment you spoke."

My heart skips a beat. This is going to shatter me into thousands of pieces if he thinks I'm someone else.

"Miss Falnor." He reaches out and brushes a finger against my cheek gently.

My breathing falters. "Yes, Mr Crestfellow?"

His lips quirk up into a smile as I reveal I know just who he is too. "Perhaps I do not need to unmask, especially as the impracticalities of wearing them are the only thing stopping me from kissing you right now."

"Then I think unmasking is a particularly bad idea," I respond. "But one in which we should engage anyway."

"I see what your sister means about your penchant for trouble."

"She is an excellent judge of that, but she also forgets that trouble can be fun." I reach up to untie my mask, the ribbons holding it in place untangling atrociously slowly.

"Allow me?" he asks.

I let my hands fall away and wordlessly turn so my back is to him.

Mr Crestfellow steps closer, and I can feel his presence in a way I've never experienced before. His deft fingers untangle the ribbons of the mask. I pull on the front of it, allowing it to slip away. I twist my neck, realising as I do that it brings our lips closer together than they've been before. He's still wearing his mask, but I don't believe I have the patience to wait for him to undo it.

I turn and reach out to cup his cheek in my hand. His eyes blaze with something unspoken and he dips forward, his lips mere inches from mine.

My eyes flutter closed and I wait for the moment he kisses me, longing for it like I never have before. I can feel his breath against my skin, and every particle of my being is yearning for more of his touch.

"Emily!"

My eyes snap open at the sound of my sister's voice, and I start running through all kinds of explanations for what she almost witnessed, though I fear that none of them will placate Mary when she is angry.

Mr Crestfellow steps back instantly, leaving me to notice the chill air that I've been ignoring from before.

I turn to my sister, able to sense how much she is seething from her glare. I'm not sure if she's angrier than she's ever been at me before, or if the mask is simply drawing more attention to her eyes, but I do know that her response is not good for me.

She hurries over and grabs my wrist, pulling me away from Mr Crestfellow. "Not a word of this to anyone," she says, warning us both.

"Of course, Your Grace," Mr Crestfellow responds, having the decency to at least seem a little embarrassed that he's being scolded by my sister. "Please accept my apologies, Miss Falnor."

"She accepts," Mary says before he has a chance to say anything else. "You should go. We'll leave in the other direction, and let's hope no one saw the two of you come in here and recognised you for who you were."

A part of me wants to ask if that's such a bad thing, but I refrain. I don't think Mary will appreciate it right now.

For a moment, I think that Mr Crestfellow is going to protest, but instead he simply nods and disappears into the maze.

Mary turns to me, and I know that this is going to be one of the worst scoldings she's ever given me. "What were you thinking?"

"I suppose I wasn't."

"Emily, this isn't the time to be flippant. Do you understand what could have happened if someone else had caught you? You're the one who has been complaining about how everyone will be able to tell who you are if you dress like a falcon, and yet you're also the one taking your mask off and almost kissing someone."

"I don't know what happened," I murmur. "We were talking, and dancing, and then it just felt right. Did that never happen with you and the Duke?"

Her face softens a little. "I suppose it did. But we weren't in this kind of situation at the time, and we knew one another a lot longer than you and Mr Crestfellow."

"Mary..." I'm not sure what I want to say, just that I know it needs to be *something*.

"We're going home," she says, starting to walk back through the maze.

I glance in the opposite direction, to where Mr Crestfellow headed, but he's already long out of sight.

"Emily," Mary says sternly.

"I'm coming." Disappointment threads through me, almost impossible for me to ignore.

I wish she hadn't come across us. Or that someone else had in her wake. With the way the night seems to be going for everyone, I doubt they'd have said anything and I would know what it felt like to kiss him.

Instead, I'm going to end up trying to fall asleep all while wondering about what could have been.

Chapter 8

EMILY

A light sprinkle of snow has fallen during the night, and I'm sad that I missed seeing it while the Shifter Yuletide Ball was still taking place, but true to her word, Mary had escorted me straight home.

And has done everything possible to keep me away from anywhere Mr Crestfellow might be ever since.

I sigh and kick my feet against the soft powderiness on the ground. All I need is a couple of minutes to speak with him. I'm not sure what I'll even say during them, but I want to know.

A bird lands a few feet away and starts to twitter, hopping up and down with excitement. I frown, wondering what's gotten it all excited.

A flash of red catches my eye and understanding dawns on me. I get to my feet and wait until the bird hops along.

A small smile twists at the corner of my lips. My sister may be good at keeping the two of us apart while we're in our human forms, but she seems to have forgotten that we have a second one.

I follow the robin until we reach a small glade of evergreen trees which effectively shield us from the house. The robin disappears behind a tree, and I step forward to follow him.

"One moment, please," Mr Crestfellow's voice calls.

My eyes widen as I realise why he needs me to wait. Clothes can't shift with us unless they're properly treated by a witch, and that makes them very expensive. Perhaps one day normal shifters will be able to afford the luxury on all of their clothing, but for now, only the Shifter Queen can.

Mr Crestfellow steps out from behind the tree, his shirt slightly in disarray, but with everything covered. "Miss Falnor..."

"I believe you've probably earned the right to call me Emily," I say.

"Only if you call me William."

"It does suit you," I admit. "William."

His face lights up as I say his name, making my

heart skip a beat in the process. It seems that the attraction I felt towards him last night was nothing to do with the magic of the ball.

"Your sister seems to be doing an admirable job at keeping me away from you," he says.

"She's good at overreacting."

He chuckles. "I don't believe the reaction is totally unwarranted. I overstepped and I shouldn't have."

"I believe it was both of us who overstepped," I point out. "I encouraged you to kiss me." I step forward without thinking about it.

"Perhaps you had drunk too much wine," he says, closing the gap even further.

"I didn't drink a drop," I promise. "Is that your excuse for what happened?"

"I have no excuse. Only reasons for why I wanted to kiss you."

"And do you still wish to now?" I'm not sure why I need to ask, we're so close together that we're almost touching, and I know it's not going to take much for us to finish what we started the night before.

"Very much so," he murmurs.

"Is it just a kiss?" The question pours from me unexpectedly.

"No."

I blink a few times, not having expected the answer.

"I know we've only known one another a short time, but it's not the desire to kiss you that has captivated me, it's the desire to know you."

"I don't want to rush into anything," I admit. "I want to properly court so we have a chance to get to know one another."

His whole face lights up as my admission of wanting the same thing sets in. "I believe that can be arranged."

"My sister may be opposed to it."

"Would you mind if I talked to her?"

"I think that would end better than if I did myself," I admit. "I don't believe she puts much faith in my judgement." And perhaps after last night, I have to concede that's fair.

"Then I will speak with her. Today."

"Thank you." I reach out and cup his cheek in my hand, recalling the way it felt last night. "Do you know where she is now?"

"I believe she is out for a ride with the Duke."

"Then there's no chance that she can stop you from kissing me this time," I respond.

"I would like nothing more."

He leans in, surprising me with just how close we already are. I suppose after falling asleep with the echo of his breath against my lips, never quite making the final move, it's inevitable that we're going to be drawn together like this.

My eyes flutter closed as his lips brush against mine and I'm rewarded with something far better than I could ever have imagined.

I wrap my arms around his neck and deepen the kiss, able to feel every nerve in my body as I do. I've flirted with plenty of gentlemen, and danced with more, but none of them have ever made me feel like this.

Perhaps it is best that Mary interrupted us last night. I may have then put it down to something as simple as the atmosphere of the ball influencing my decisions and making me do irrational things. But today, I'm certain that's not what it is at all.

The connection I feel to Mr Cr-William, might be new, but it could lead to something special, and I'm certain of it.

Convincing Mary will be the hard part, but I'm sure we can manage, especially if there's the threat of us being discovered by others on the line.

We break apart and I lift my fingers to my lips, the slight tingle of his touch against them lingering there. It was even better than I dreamed, and I don't want to have to give that up.

The sound of horses galloping down the path causes our attention to stray from one another.

"I should get back to the house lest Mary suspect anything," I say.

William nods. "I'll speak with her this afternoon."

"I wish you the best of luck." I go up on my toes and press a kiss against his cheek. I head away from the trees, looking over my shoulder a couple of times to try and catch a glimpse of him.

William raises his hand to wave at me and I feel a wave of happiness spread through me as a result.

Perhaps my unannounced trip to Mary's new house is going to end even better than I expected it to.

Chapter 9

WILLIAM

I don't believe I've ever felt so uncomfortable sitting opposite anyone, and that includes my step-mother when she's having one of her bad days, but there's something intimidating about sitting opposite Emily's sister, even when she's pouring tea and doing her best to appear as the best hostess she possibly can.

"Here you are, Mr Crestfellow," she says, handing me the teacup.

"Thank you, Your Grace." I take it from her and add a lump of sugar along with some cream.

"I have to admit that I'm rather perplexed about why you wish to speak with me," she says, almost with a hint of warning in her voice.

She is probably well aware of what I want to

talk to her about. Which is a good reason to get straight to it and not prolong the torture for longer than we need to.

"It is about your sister," I say slowly.

She stiffens. "I would rather we forgot about the whole thing. I understand that these things happen."

"I can not forget it."

"You should, Mr Crestfellow. I don't wish for my sister to be trapped in a loveless marriage."

"Neither do I, Your Grace."

She raises an eyebrow. "Have you known one another long enough to call it love?"

"I make no such assertions," I promise. "But I do believe that what we feel could grow into love."

"That is too great of a risk, I can not allow a marriage to go ahead on the promise that there may be love in the future."

"I understand that. I only wish to start a courtship. As the three of us, and presumably the Duke, are the only ones aware of what transpired last night, I see no reason for Miss Falnor and I to rush to the altar." Even though I've never said her given name out loud, it still feels wrong to call her by her surname, especially to her sister.

"That is a relief."

"I'm aware that your father is no longer in this world, and that it is your permission I would need in order to court Miss Falnor."

"I rather think it is Emily's permission you require," she says with a hint of amusement.

"I believe I already have that," I admit.

"From last night? Or did the two of you find a way to cross paths this morning?"

"The latter." I see no point in lying to her, especially if I intend for our courtship to end in marriage.

"I see." She sighs. "I do not know what Emily has told you of our situation."

"She said that your father had left you both money that couldn't be controlled by your husbands."

"She has been rather talkative, I see." The affection is clear from the way she says it. "She doesn't have a dowry."

"That should not be a problem, particularly should she have money of her own. I'm the heir to my father's estates, and while they are certainly no match for a Dukedom, I believe they will provide a decent income for the two of us and any children we would eventually have."

"It is not your money that concerns me, nor any

title," the Duchess says. "I simply wish for my sister to be happy. She has been trapped in a situation that isn't much to her liking, and I would like to free her from that."

"You do not believe a courtship will do that?"

"I believe that you may find obstacles in your path, namely our aunt. She does not wish to give up the retainer she gets for being my sister's keeper. Stephen is trying what he can to fix the situation, but I am not hopeful."

"I will do whatever I can to help," I promise.

"Then you have my blessing to court Emily, but only so long as she allows it. If she says one word to the contrary, I will ruin your good standing in society and you will never again be able to set foot at any shifter events." The expression on her face says that she means it, and gives me a glimpse into what my friend sees in her. She's a formidable Duchess, even if I'm sure she feels she has some learning to do.

"Thank you, Your Grace."

"Don't hurt my sister, please. She and Stephen are all I have." The rawness in her voice is impossible to miss.

"I have no intention of doing so."

"Good." She rises to her feet. "I should go, I

have errands to run. Knowing Emily, you'll find her trying to listen in on the other side of the door." She gestures to it.

Curious, I rise to my feet. I open the door only to find Emily jumping back.

An amused snort comes from the Duchess, but I ignore her. There's only one of the sisters I wish to talk to right in this moment.

"If you expect me to be listening, then I did nothing wrong," Emily says defiantly.

"That is interesting logic," the Duchess responds.

"You're truly not going to stand in the way of us courting?" Emily asks, looking past me.

"If it is what you desire, then no, I won't stand in the way. Though I will intervene should I consider the two of you being improper at a ball again."

"But not if we are improper in other places?"

The Duchess lets out a small groan of frustration. "Just try not to get caught."

"I'm not sure I'm going to be able to do that," Emily says, looking up at me and smiling.

"Then at least make sure I leave the room first," the Duchess responds, walking past the two of us and touching Emily's arm briefly in what I think is a reassuring gesture.

"She truly said we can court?" Emily asks me once we are alone, giving weight to the Duchess' insistence that we simply not get caught.

"Yes."

Emily lets out an excited squeal and steps closer.

I wrap my arms around her and close the distance between us. I capture her lips with mine and kiss her for the second wonderful time.

I don't know what the future holds for us, but I hope that is more of this.

Epilogue
EMILY

One Year Later

I REACH up and touch my hair, making sure the elaborate strands are still in place. Despite knowing that everything is properly above board, a part of me is nervous about the bright red plume that is nestled between the brown feathers of a falcon. It isn't seen as strange to wear a husband's feather to the Shifter Yuletide Ball, and yet I'm nervous about it.

"You look beautiful," William assures me as our carriage pulls to a stop.

"You have to say that, you're my husband."

"And as I once told you, I believe that every lady is beautiful."

"Which is probably something you shouldn't say to your wife," I point out.

"Ah, but my wife knows that I always find her to be the most beautiful in the room."

Despite knowing he's trying to be charming, my heart melts a little. "I'm looking forward to dancing with you tonight," I admit. "We haven't been able to do that in six months."

"Would you give up six months of marriage in order to dance with me again at a ball?"

"You know I would not. But I do enjoy that there are no rules at this ball."

"Is your sister aware of that?" he asks, an amused smile on his face.

"The Duke and Duchess are too close to the birth of their first child to be attending this evening," I remind him. "It does not matter what my sister deems appropriate."

He chuckles good-naturedly. "Then I suspect the best course of events will be to dance, and then find our way to the rather lovely maze where all of this began."

"I believe that sounds agreeable." I smile at him.

"Did you truly know that it was me when you approached me last year?"

"Not when I approached you," he responds. "But the moment you spoke, I did. And I felt like I should have known the entire time. When did you realise?"

"Around the same moment. Though I had been watching you for much longer. I'm glad to see you've chosen to wear the red waistcoat again." I reach out and touch the fabric over his chest.

"How could I not when you seemed to love it so?"

"It makes you my Lord Redbreast." I can feel my face aching from my smiles, but I can't help it. Everything turned out so perfectly.

"I fear you may have come to care for me too much to remain Lady Wit," he jests. "Perhaps I should rename you."

"I don't believe that will be necessary. I'll have you know that I've been saving several rather witty remarks, especially for tonight."

"I look forward to hearing them." He takes my gloved hand in his and smoothes his thumb over the back of it. "I love you, Emily. I think I have from the moment we met."

"I love you too," I respond. "Though I believe it

took a little longer than that." But not by much. Our courtship only lasted up until six months before the wedding because Mary kept wanting to make sure I was certain about it. I would have married William much sooner.

The carriage rolls to a stop, announcing our arrival at the ball that started it all. And I couldn't be more pleased to be returning.

Thank you for reading *The Dancer and the Robin*, I hope you enjoyed it! If you want to learn more about Mary and the Duke's romance, you can in *The Falcon and the Bluestocking:* https://books.authorlauragreenwood.co.uk/thefalconandthebluestocking

Or you can start the series at the beginning with *The Fox and the Viscount*: https://books.authorlauragreenwood.co.uk/thefoxandtheviscount

Author Note

Thank you for reading *The Dancer and the Robin*, I hope you enjoyed it! And to those of you who are reading this as my 2022 Christmas Freebie (a yearly tradition for readers in my Facebook Reader Group & on my mailing list!) Happy Holidays!

If you want to know more about Emily's sister, Mary, then you can in *The Falcon and the Bluestocking*. Several of the other briefly mentioned characters from the ball scene also have their own books - Lady Cygnus/Miss Swanley in *The Swan and the Rake*, Georgiana in *The Otter and the Officer*, the Renartons in *The Fox and the Viscount*, the Peaburys in *The Peacock and the Wallflower*, and Lady Ferrington in *The Stag and the Baroness*. If this is your first introduction to *The Shifter Season* series, then you might have guessed that it's two of my favourite genres combined - paranormal romance and Regency romance. It's a passion-project series of mine that I've been incredibly grateful for the support of readers for!

Sometimes, coming up with the perfect character name is hard (particularly when you need to check it existed and was used in a certain era!) and sometimes, characters name themselves. Emily is one of the latter, and, having lived with two Emilys (at the same time), I should have known what that meant for the character herself. I care deeply for both the Emilys in my life, and that made me feel extra affectionate towards book-Emily too - just as it has done when I've had characters named after other people I've known in real life! I've never intended to name a character after someone real, but as I said, sometimes, characters just name themselves and no matter how many times you try, no other name fits them quite right. Sadly, neither of the Emilys are falcon shifters, and one of them did once ask whether birds have arms, which potentially puts her out of contention - or maybe she was just trying to put us off the scent of the truth! (Emily, if you're reading this, sorry!)

If you want to keep up to date with new releases and other news, you can join my Facebook Reader Group or mailing list.

Stay safe & happy reading!

- Laura

Also by Laura Greenwood

You can find out more about each of my series on my website.

- Obscure Academy: a paranormal romance series set at a university-age academy for mixed supernaturals. Each book follows a different couple.
- The Apprentice Of Anubis: an urban fantasy series set in an alternative world where the Ancient Egyptian Empire never fell. It follows a new apprentice to the temple of Anubis as she learns about her new role.
- Forgotten Gods: a paranormal adventure romance series inspired by Egyptian mythology. Each book follows a different Ancient Egyptian goddess.
- Amethyst's Wand Shop Mysteries (with Arizona Tape): an urban fantasy murder mystery series following a witch who teams up with a detective to solve murders. Each book includes a different murder.
- Grimm Academy: a fantasy fairy tale academy series. Each book follows a different fairy tale heroine.

- Jinx Paranormal Dating Agency: a paranormal romance series based on worldwide mythology where paranormals and deities take part in events organised by the Jinx Dating Agency. Each book follows a different couple.
- Purple Oasis (with Arizona Tape): a paranormal romance series based at a sanctuary set up after the apocalypse. Each book follows a different couple.
- Speed Dating With The Denizens Of The Underworld (shared world): a paranormal romance shared world based on mythology from around the world. Each book follows a different couple.
- Blackthorn Academy For Supernaturals (shared world): a paranormal monster romance shared world based at Blackthorn Academy. Each book follows a different couple.

You can find a complete list of all my books on my website:

https://books.authorlauragreenwood.co.uk/book-list

Signed Paperback & Merchandise:

You can find signed paperbacks, hardcovers, and

merchandise based on my series (including stickers, magnets, face masks, and more!) via my website:

https://books.authorlauragreenwood.co.uk/shop

About Laura Greenwood

Laura is a USA Today Bestselling Author of paranormal romance, urban fantasy, and fantasy romance. When she's not writing, she drinks a lot of tea, tries to resist French macarons, and works towards a diploma in Egyptology. She lives in the UK, where most of her books are set. Laura specialises in quick reads, with healthy relationships and consent-positive moments regardless of if she's writing light-hearted romance, mythology-heavy urban fantasy, or anything in between.

Follow Laura Greenwood

- Website: www.authorlaura-greenwood.co.uk
- Mailing List: https://books.authorlauragreenwood.co.uk/newsletter
- Facebook Group: http://facebook.com/groups/theparanormalcouncil
- Facebook Page: http://facebook.com/authorlauragreenwood

- Bookbub: https://www.bookbub.com/authors/laura-greenwood

www.ingramcontent.com/pod-product-compliance
Lightning Source LLC
Chambersburg PA
CBHW021338160726

47994CB00007B/2751